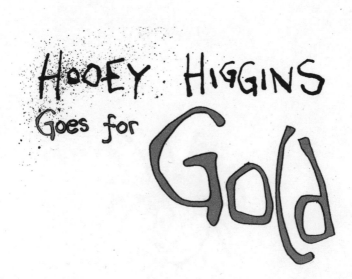

HOOEY HIGGINS
Goes for Gold

For Ben
S.V.

For Zakaria
E.D.

COMING
SOON:

HOOEY
HIGGINS
AND THE
BIG DAY
OUT

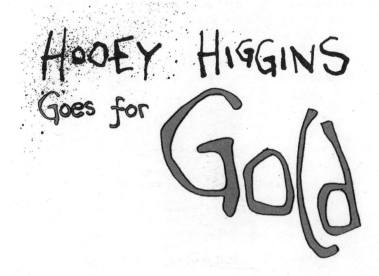

HOOEY HIGGINS
Goes for Gold

STEVE VOAKE

illustrated by Emma Dodson

WALKER
BOOKS

This is a work of fiction. Names, characters, places and incidents
are either the product of the author's imagination or, if real,
used fictitiously. All statements, activities, stunts, descriptions,
information and material of any other kind contained herein are
included for entertainment purposes only and should not be
relied on for accuracy or replicated as they may result in injury.

First published 2012 by Walker Books Ltd
87 Vauxhall Walk, London SE11 5HJ

2 4 6 8 10 9 7 5 3 1

Text © 2012 Steve Voake
Illustrations © 2012 Emma Dodson

This book has been typeset in StempelSchneidler and EDodson

Printed and bound in Great Britain
by Clays Ltd, St Ives plc

British Library Cataloguing in Publication Data:
a catalogue record for this book is available from the British Library

ISBN 978-1-4063-2241-5

www.walker.co.uk

CONTENTS

GREECE IS THE WORD

"This term," said Miss Troutson, pointing to a picture of a man in a tunic, "our project is about Ancient Greece."

"I could get my cousin Nigel in," whispered Twig. *"His hair's full of it."*

"What we need is facts," continued Miss Troutson, stabbing at the air with her finger. "Facts, facts, facts. So, come on. Who's going to start us off?"

On the other side of the room, Basbo shoved up his hand as if he was punching a parachutist in the wotchamacallits.

"Yes Barry?"

"My mum's got the CD, innit?"

"I'm sorry, Barry, I don't quite—"

Greece izza word izza word izza word—

"I think he's talking about *Grease* the musical," said Sarah-Jane Silverton, who went to singing lessons and knew about such things.

"Thassit," said Basbo, thumping his fist on the table. "Greece izza word izza word izza word—"

"Well it *is* a word, Barry," agreed Miss Troutson, "but just for now I would very much like you to stop saying it."

Basbo folded his arms and growled at Twig.

"Why's he looking at me?" asked Twig. "I didn't do anything."

"Don't take it personally," said Hooey. "He probably just wants to kill someone."

"Now then," said Miss Troutson, looking around the room. "Has anyone got a *sensible* suggestion?"

Samantha Curbitt put her hand up.

"Yes Samantha?"

"The Ancient Greeks lived over two thousand years ago. They wrote plays and did maths and invented things."

"Sounds like your brother Will," whispered Twig. "He's not Greek, is he?"

"Not as far as I know," said Hooey. "Although he did break some plates once.. And he likes taramasalata."

Twig frowned. "What, those big hairy spiders?"

Hooey suddenly realized the room had gone quiet.

"Ex*cuse* me," said Miss Troutson, staring at Twig. "Have you actually listened to a single word I've said?"

Hooey quickly scribbled **Ancient Greece** on a piece of paper and slid it across the table towards Twig.

"Ankee-ent Grecky," said Twig confidently, reading from the piece of paper. "You were talking about Ankee-ent Grecky."

Ancient Greece

Miss Troutson went red in the face and Hooey decided to help Twig out before she took him outside and flushed his head down the toilet.

"Umm, Miss Troutson?"

"Yes Hooey, what is it?"

"What Twig's *trying* to say is that, because the Ancient Greeks invented the Olympics, we could try and find out more about them."

To Hooey's relief, Miss Troutson seemed rather keen on this idea.

"I'm glad you mentioned the Olympics," she said, "because that brings me on to my very special surprise."

At the word SURPRISE, everyone sat bolt upright in their seats. Although it was unlikely to be free sweets or exploding teachers, there was still a chance it might be good.

"Wazzitt?" asked Basbo. "Wazzigonnbee?"

"If you just listen for a moment, Barry," said Miss Troutson, "I might actually tell you."

Basbo sat back and gnawed his knuckles.

Everyone else leaned forward, except for Twig, who was so excited he went cross-eyed and forgot to breathe.

"Mr Papadopoulos, the manager of the local Greek restaurant, has agreed to sponsor some special Olympic events at next week's Sports Day."

"Rare," said Twig, remembering to breathe again.

Double decent!

"Wait," said Miss Troutson, "there's more. Mr Papadopoulos has also said the winner of each event will get a special gold medal in recognition of their achievement."

To gasps of amazement, Miss Troutson held up a blue and white ribbon with a gold medal dangling from the end of it.

"*Look*," whispered Twig as beams of light reflected from its surface. *"It's like buried treasure, only not buried."*

"We are SO winning one of those," said Hooey.

Miss Troutson peered at the medal through her glasses. "Sarah-Jane, can you come up and read this for me please? The writing's rather small."

"Certainly, Miss Troutson," said Sarah-Jane, holding the medal up to the light. "It says: WINNER OF THE SHRIMPTON-ON-SEA GAMES. And on the back it says … FOR A GOLDEN DINING EXPERIENCE, VISIT ZORBA'S RESTAURANT."

"Right," said Miss Troutson. "Jolly good."

"I could be in a race!" said Twig excitedly. "I could be an Ancient Greek!"

"Ancient Geek, you mean," said Wayne.

"Ignore him," said Hooey, patting Twig's arm. "When I've trained you up, you'll be the best athlete Shrimpton has ever seen. What do you think of that then, Twiggy-boy?"

Twig's eyes glazed over as if he could already see himself on the winner's podium. "Greece," he said dreamily, "izza word."

There was a loud **crunch** as a pencil case struck him in the centre of his forehead. "**Blam!**" shouted Basbo as Twig fell off his chair. "**Snotchoresong. Smysong!**"

"*Really,* Barry," said Miss Troutson, helping Twig up from beneath the table. "That is *not* the way to behave." Basbo thumped the side of his head with his fist. "Well you've obviously got a strong right hand," she added.

Shall I put you down for the welly-throwing competition?

DALEY
DECATHLON

Hooey's brother Will was in the library, busily sketching out plans on a roll of wallpaper.

"Hi Will," said Hooey. "Wotcha doin'?"

"Designing a Gerball," said Will.

"A gerbil?"

"No, a Ger*ball*."

Hooey peered over Will's shoulder and saw that he had drawn a picture of a football swerving round a goalkeeper. On the sidelines, a small boy was holding a box with an aerial sticking out of it.

"It's a radio-controlled football," Will explained. "Helps you bend banana shots into the back of the net."

"Nice," said Twig.

Will had drawn a diagram showing the inside of the ball with an arrow pointing at some trapdoors. He had written the words

tasty snacks

tasty snacks and underneath it three gerbils were staring up expectantly.

Hooey frowned. "What's with the gerbils, Will?"

"They're for steering purposes," said Will. "When you push the lever, a trapdoor opens and a tasty snack falls out. The gerbils run over and the shift of weight makes the ball swerve. You can do it either way, left or right."

"Won't they get hurt?" asked Hooey.

"Not with these special Shockproof Suits," said Will.

He handed
Hooey a picture
of a gerbil wearing
clumpy shoes,
shoulder pads and
a helmet. Its
whiskers were
poking through the helmet
guard and it was smiling and giving the
thumbs-up.

Hooey stared at the drawings in
admiration.

As usual, Will
seemed to have
thought of everything.

"Um, Will, while
you're busy thinking
up stuff, can you help
us train Twig for the
Olympics?"

"Shouldn't be a problem," said Will, as though he got asked that kind of thing all the time. "How long have we got?"

"About three days."

"Three days? Are you sure?"

"It's the Shrimpton-on-Sea Olympics," said Hooey. "Sponsored by Mr Papadopoulos."

"Will should eat some brain food to help him think of stuff," suggested Twig. "Taramasalata, maybe."

"Will doesn't need brain food," said Hooey. "His brain is already the size of a planet. Let's leave him to it and find out more about the events."

"How about this?" suggested Twig, picking up a book from the shelf.

Hooey looked at it and put it back again. "That's a book about limpets, Twig. We're supposed to be finding out about the Olympics."

"I'm sure she said 'limpets'."

"Twig, why would she ask us to find out about limpets? We're doing a topic about the Ancient Greeks."

"Well they like taramasalata, and that's fishy stuff."

"*So?*"

"Limpets are fishy."

"Twig, just shut up about limpets."

Hooey picked up a book called *The History of the Modern Olympics.* Inside was a photograph of a man called Daley Thompson. He was holding a javelin and smiling at the camera.

"Ooh," said Twig. "Is that the Queen?"

"No Twig, it's not the Queen. It's a man called Daley Thompson. He won two gold medals at the Olympics."

"What, just for chucking a spear?"

"He had to do nine other things as well. But I expect he got to have a sandwich or something in between."

"I'd have cheese and pickle," said Twig. "No, wait. Cheese and marmalade. No. Peanut butter."

"Probably best not to get too hung up on sandwiches at this stage," said Hooey. "Daley doesn't really mention them, to be honest. He says success is about having the will to win."

Twig looked over at Will and grinned. "We're halfway there then," he said.

In the corner of the library, Basbo suddenly opened a pop-up book of the human body and screamed.

A cardboard skull had appeared unexpectedly and he punched it to the floor before jumping up and down on it.

Skurpy-skellig!

he shouted. "Bashiminna bonioes an frampiminna froonies!"

"Basbo seems a bit on edge today," said Hooey.

"Maybe he's training for a new event," said Twig.

"What, Smash It In The Face And Ask Questions Later?" asked Will.

"He'd win that without trying," said Twig. "But how am *I* going to get one of those medals? I can't do any of that stuff."

"In that case," said Hooey, "you've just got to ask yourself: What would Daley Thompson do?" He picked up the book and began thumbing through the pages. "Ah, here we are: Inspirational Quotes by Daley Thompson. Number One: IF YOU'RE NOT IN IT, YOU CAN'T WIN IT."

"That's not true," said Twig. "My Uncle Ernie won a paddling pool once and he definitely wasn't in it. He was on holiday in Torremolinos."

"OK," said Hooey, turning the page, "here's another one.

Daley says, BEING A DECATHLETE IS LIKE
HAVING TEN GIRLFRIENDS. YOU HAVE
TO LOVE THEM ALL, AND YOU CAN'T
AFFORD TO LOSE ONE."

"Eh?"

"Not my words, Twig," said Hooey, tapping
the page with his finger. "The words of Daley
Thompson, double gold medal winner."

"Perhaps we should scale it down a
bit for him," suggested Will. "Maybe
one gold medal, one girlfriend."

"But I don't want a girlfriend," said Twig.

"Of course you don't," said Hooey. "Although I know a little someone who might be impressed if you won a medal."

Twig blushed. "Are you talking about Samantha?"

"Everyone likes a bit of gold, Twig. All we need to do is pick an event and use our skill and expertise to make sure you succeed."

Twig frowned. "But I haven't got any skill or ... that other thing you said."

"Not a problem," said Hooey. "Will?"

Will unrolled some fresh wallpaper and nodded.

2×9

3×9

1×9

GOLD!

UNIDENTIFIED FLYING OBJECTS

On the other side of the library, Basbo picked up a book about UFOs and stared at it upside down.

"Spacey-bams," he muttered. "Spacey-bams unn moony-men."

"I like it when he's reading," said Twig. "It means he's not trying to kill me."

"Twig, you've got to concentrate," said Hooey, looking at his list. "We need to find an event that you can win. How about the Shot-Put?"

"What's that?"

"It's where you put one of those big heavy balls under your chin."

"Like the ones on cranes?"

"Smaller. You put it under your chin and go **Huh!**"

"Ooh, I like that," said Twig happily. "**Huh!**"

Hooey looked at him. "You can't just make the noise, Twig. You have to throw it as well."

"All right, skip that one. What else?"

"There's the Discus, which is a bit like throwing a plate."

"I could do that," said Twig. He picked up the cheese plant

that stood in the corner of the library and
took the china plate out from underneath.
He held it between finger and thumb and
pretended to throw it.

"Not like that,"
said Hooey.
"Like this."

He turned the
plate over, placed his
palm on top and
gripped the edge
with his fingers. Then
he held his arm out
and swivelled his hips,
swinging the plate back
and forth as he did so.

"You see? You just
keep swinging it until you get up to full
power and then BAM! The discus flies
off and you win the gold."

"Shweet," said Twig. He held the plate at arm's length and moved the top half of his body, swinging the plate back and forth in a semi-circle.

"That's it," said Hooey. "Now you're getting the hang of it."

Twig began to giggle. "I'm doing it!" he shouted,

swinging his arms harder and harder
until he was spinning around in a circle.
"Whey-hey!"

"Take it easy, Twig," said Hooey as Twig's
face blurred past for the fifth time. "I think
you're going too—"

Before he could say the word "fast",
Twig lost his footing, fell into a table
and the plate flew out of his hand.

"Oops," he said as it shot off across the library. The librarian, Mrs Gumbleton, who was carrying a large pile of books across to her office, heard a faint whooshing sound.

Basbo heard it too and peered over the top of his book. Seeing a strange white object skimming across the tables towards him,

he glanced back at the pictures of the flying saucers in his book.

Then something smacked him very hard in the forehead, knocked him off his chair and sent him flying into the arms of Mrs Gumbleton. With a cry of **"NON-FICTION!"** she crashed into a shelving unit and fell to the floor, closely followed by fifteen books, several bits of broken china and a large, stubble-headed boy.

As a small pot plant wobbled, fell off the top shelf and smashed onto Basbo's head, Hooey turned to Twig and gave him a disapproving look. "You see what happens when you don't stick to the training plan?" he said.

Basbo sat up, brushed earth from his head and stared at the broken plate. Then he stared at Twig.

"**Uh-oh**," said Twig.

"Just act like you didn't do anything."

"I didn't," said Hooey. "You did."

Nervously, Twig picked up a book and pretended to read. "Well would you believe it?" he said. "Apparently limpets

were invented by Daley Thompson in lemteen hundred and lemty-lem."

"Forget it, Twig," said Hooey. "He's coming over."

Twig peered over his book and saw Basbo advancing across the library towards him.

"RIGHT, Y'LITTLE GRIMBLESHANKS," he roared, shaking his fist, "I'M GONNA CRIMBALIZE YER CRANKIES AND FRAMP YOU IN THE FRINKLENUTS!"

Eek!

With a small squeak, Twig ran out into the corridor with Basbo's footsteps thumping across the carpet behind him.

"Hey! Come back!" shouted Mrs Gumbleton from beneath the pile of books. "The books are on my face! This is not where they go! This is not where they go at all!"

But Basbo wasn't coming back for anyone.

As Twig burst through the doors into the playground, everyone ran to the windows to watch.

"SMASHIMINNA BRIMBLES!" shouted Basbo. "WHOPPIMINNA WOOBEREES!"

At that moment, Mrs Bilks appeared from behind the PE shed pushing a trolley full of cabbages. She was so busy thinking about boiling them up for school dinners that she didn't notice Twig and Basbo running

towards her. Nor did she notice Mr Bilks
the caretaker crossing the playground with
a wheelbarrow full of manure.

Twig noticed both of these things and
hoped that he'd be able to stop in time.
The children at the windows noticed them
too and very much hoped that he wouldn't.

"BASHIM INNA BINGERTONS!"
shouted Basbo. "CRACKIMINNA
CROOPONS!"

MIND MY
CABBAGES!

shouted Mrs Bilks.

45

At the last moment, Twig leapt into the air and hung suspended above the cabbages before landing with a thump in front of Mr Bilks's manure-filled wheelbarrow. Realizing he was going too fast to stop, Twig jumped like a jackrabbit and cleared the top of the wheelbarrow by almost half a metre.

"YAY!" shouted the children at the windows, banging on the glass and rattling the window frames.

"Phew," said Mrs Billks as Twig hit the fence and fell over. "That was close." At which point Basbo slammed into the side of the trolley and sent her cabbages rolling and bouncing across the playground.

"OH MR BILKS!," she cried. "It's a CABBAGE CATASTROPHE!"

"What the—?" said Mr Bilks, gripping the handles of his wheelbarrow as Basbo danced across the cabbages like a monkey wearing roller skates.

Mrs Bilks covered her eyes.

Then Basbo's feet
slipped off the last cabbage
and with a sound like
a spade on wet cement
he hit the manure with
such force that the fallout
splashed Mr Bilks from
head to toe and covered
the wall in a gooey
brown sludge.

Eeeeeyewwww!

cried the children inside
the classrooms, jumping
backwards as wet
manure splattered
the windows.

Slowly, like some strange mud-dwelling monster, Basbo raised himself from the wheelbarrow and pointed at Twig with a pooey finger. "**Graaaaagggh!**" he shouted. "**Grrreeeeeerrrgh!**"

Twig nodded sympathetically.

"I can see you're upset," he said. "But one day you'll look back on this and laugh."

Basbo climbed out of the wheelbarrow and squeezed his fists until his knuckles cracked.

"Or … maybe not," said Twig.

Then he ran.

MONSTERS AND MEDALS

"Look on the bright side," said Hooey as they walked home from school. "That plate would have gone for miles if Basbo's head hadn't been in the way. And your wheelbarrow jump had gold medal performance written all over it."

"Look on the dark side," said Twig. "I can't win a gold medal if Basbo rips my head off."

"He won't rip your head off," said Hooey. "He'll probably use a saw or something."

"Very funny," said Twig.

"Anyway, Daley Thompson says it's important to always think positive," said Hooey.

"Try telling that to Basbo," said Twig. "I mean, what's positive about having a plate smashed over your head?"

Hooey thought for a moment.

"It gives him something to write about in his diary."

When Hooey got home, Grandpa was slicing bread and Dingbat was clearing up the crumbs.

"Fancy a toastie?" asked Grandpa.

"You bet," said Hooey, dumping his school bag in the corner. Dingbat promptly sat on it, curled up and went to sleep.

"He must have had a tough day," said Hooey, "what with getting up and eating and going back to sleep again."

"Bit like being
retired," said Grandpa.
He sprinkled some grated cheese
between two slices of toast, squashed
them together and handed it
to Hooey. "There," he said.
"That'll keep your
strength up."

"What *is* the best food for keeping your strength up, Grandpa?" asked Hooey.

"Depends what for," said Grandpa.

"Winning the Olympics, mainly."

"Ah," said Grandpa. "In that case I'd suggest some good home-cooking."

Hooey took a bite of his toastie and remembered that Twig's home-cooking usually consisted of a sausage roll, two bags of crisps and a bottle of cola. Which was OK if you just wanted to run around being dopey, but not so OK if you wanted to win a gold medal. Hooey decided that Twig's diet was an area that needed attention.

"Did you do any sport when you were younger, Grandpa?"

"Oh, we used to do a bit of cheese-rolling," said Grandpa, shaking ketchup onto his toastie. "I was pretty good at it actually."

"What's cheese-rolling?"

"Same as it sounds. You take a wheel of cheese up to the top of a hill and let go of it. Then everyone chases it down to the bottom. It's a bit mad really."

Hooey watched Grandpa stare into space and guessed his cheese-rolling days must have been fun.

"Was it an *Olympic* sport?"

Grandpa chuckled. "No, but it should have been. I reckon by the time we got to the bottom we were running faster than any of those fellas in their fancy shorts and trainers."

"Did you win?"

"Two years in a row. I was only beaten the third time when I saw your grandma flying down the hill next to me. I took my eye off the cheese for a second and we crashed into a chestnut tree. Woke up to the sound of conkers falling on my head. But your grandma was there next to me, which is pretty much where she's been ever since." Grandpa winked at Hooey. "Should've kept my eye on that cheese, eh?"

Hooey smiled. "So who won?"

"My old friend Theo Papadopoulos, who had just moved to Shrimpton. He runs the Greek restaurant in town. No one could ever beat him and everyone reckoned it was because he lived on the food of the original Greek champions."

"The food of champions," whispered Hooey. *"Of course!"*

Picking up a pen, he made a note of it on the back of his hand.

"Thanks, Grandpa. You've been a great help."

"Have I?" said Grandpa, scratching his head. Then he sliced two more pieces of bread, popped them in the toaster and thought fondly back to the days when he was the CHAMPION CHEESE-ROLLER OF SHRIMPTON-ON-SEA.

Will was sitting at his desk, drawing on the back of wallpaper. "I've been thinking up some training techniques to prepare Twig for the Hundred Metres," he said. "Want to see?"

"Sure," said Hooey.

Will handed Hooey a drawing
of a boy running away
from a fierce-looking
monster with snakes
coming out of its head.

"It's Medusa," he explained,
"a gorgon from the Greek myths. It's
also an excellent training aid to help
athletes reach their top speed in the shortest
possible time."

Hooey frowned. "How's that work then?"

"Well let me put it this way: if you saw
one of these, what would you do?"

"Wet myself probably."

"OK. And then?"

"Run away as fast as I could."

"Exactly!" said
Will.

"I can see where you're coming from," said Hooey, "but I can also see a slight problem."

"Go on."

"Gorgons don't actually exist, do they?"

Will sighed. "I *know* they don't exist, Hooey. I'm just using it to illustrate my point."

"Which is?"

"FEAR. We might not have any actual Greek monsters, but there are lots of other ways to scare people into running faster. It's like when you touch something hot, your natural reaction is to pull away from it as fast as you can."

"You mean we could set fire to Twig's shorts?"

"In theory, yes – although I think they've got rules against that kind of thing, so we could probably only use it in training. When are you seeing him next?"

"Tomorrow morning. I'm going to sort out his diet."

"OK," said Will. "You work on that side of things and then later on we can put our training programme into practice. How does that sound?"

Hooey smiled.

"It sounds like a gold medal," he said.

Like a gold medal with our name on it.

CHEESE OF CHAMPIONS

The sign above the window of the restaurant said:

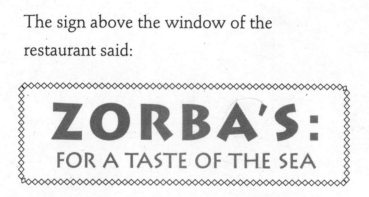

ZORBA'S:
FOR A TASTE OF THE SEA

"Probably uses a lot of salt," said Twig.

Hooey rang the bell and after a few moments the door opened to reveal Mr Papadopoulos – a small, dark-haired man who wore a big chef's hat and an even bigger smile.

"Hello boys!" he said. "You are hungry, yes?" He shook his head sadly. "Me too, me too. You have breakfast and then, **boom!** ten minutes later you are hungry again. And you know why?"

Hooey and Twig shook their heads.

"Because the food I make is so bee-yootiful. All the time it call to me, saying, 'Give me a home! Make me happy!' But always it must wait until the restaurant is open."

He looked back into the restaurant and shouted, "BE QUIET, ALL OF YOU! When we open tonight there will be homes for you all!"

"Is he talking to his food?" whispered Twig.

"I think he is," said Hooey.

"Now tell me," said Mr Papadopoulos, turning back to face them, "what can I do for you?"

"We've come to ask your advice," said Hooey. "About food."

"Well why didn't you say so?" cried Mr Papadopoulos, clapping his hands together and ushering them inside. "Come in! Come in!"

"Grandpa told me you beat him in a cheese-rolling contest," said Hooey as they sat at a table covered with a crisp white cloth.

"Ah yes," said Mr Papadopoulos, straightening up the cutlery in front of him. "The great cheese-rolling contest of 1958. I remember it as if it were yesterday."

Twig frowned and checked the date on his watch.

"The thing is, Mr Papadopoulos," said Hooey, ignoring Twig, "you've eaten Greek food all your life, haven't you?"

"Why eat anything else?" asked Mr Papadopoulos, scrunching the fingers of his right hand together and kissing the tips. "It is the food of champions!"

"That's what I thought," said Hooey. "And if Twig's going to win a gold medal, he needs to eat the right food."

"Who's Twig?" asked Mr Papadopoulos.

"I am," said Twig.

Mr Papadopoulos looked at Twig, and then back at Hooey. "Are you sure?"

Hooey nodded. "I know he doesn't look much like a champion at the moment, but that's only because we haven't trained him up yet. If you can help us with his diet, I think we're on to a winner."

Mr Papadopoulos looked at Twig again. Then he stood up, took his chef's hat off the table and placed it back on his head. "Wait," he said.

I shall return!

A few minutes later he came back with two bowls on a tray. He picked up the first bowl and placed it in front of Twig.

"These are olives," said Mr Papadopoulos, "filled with the oil that gives strength and happiness to all who eat it."

"Oil?" said Twig. "What, like in a car?"

"No," said Mr Papadopoulos, "like in an olive."

Twig popped one in his mouth, chewed for a bit and then swallowed. "Mmm, not bad. Bit hard in the middle though."

Mr Papadopoulos smiled and patted Twig so heartily on the back that the olive stone flew out and hit the bowl with a loud ting.

"Feta," said Mr Papadopoulos, placing the second bowl on the table.

"Much better thank you," said Twig, patting his stomach.

"No, *feta*," repeated Mr Papadopoulos. "Feta cheese, made from the milk of sheep which live in the fields around Athens. Do you know what that means?"

"That they haven't got any cows?"

"No. It means they are descended from the same sheep that made cheese for the very first Olympic athletes."

Mr Papadopoulos stood up and clenched his fists in front of him. "What you are looking at here, my friend, is the Cheese of Champions!"

"*The cheese of champions,*" whispered Hooey.

Twig popped a chunk in his mouth and chewed.

Hooey and Mr Papadopoulos exchanged anxious glances.

"Well?" asked Mr Papadopoulos when Twig had swallowed it.

"Bit salty," said Twig.

"But how do you *feel*?" asked Mr Papadopoulos, slapping his chest. "In *here*?"

Twig smiled.

I feel like a champion.

BACON BUTTY

"Do you really think cheese will make me a champion?" asked Twig.

"Should do," said Hooey. "Mr Papadopoulos ate some just before he won the cheese-rolling contest."

"He likes cheese, doesn't he?"

"Loves it. Said he wanted cheese-rolling to be one of the events next week, but the school wouldn't allow it. Something to do with **HEALTH AND SAFETY**. He'd had an extra medal made and everything."

"Oh well," said Twig. "As my Uncle Ernie used to say, life's not all about cheese."

Hooey frowned.

"Didn't he used to work on the cheese counter at Tesco?"

"Only during the week. On Saturdays he had a cheese stall at the market."

"Right," said Hooey. "So actually his life was quite a lot about cheese."

"Not really," said Twig. "On Sundays he used to take the day off to visit his nan."

"Where did she live?"

When they reached the school playing field, Will was standing next to the running track, holding a book in one hand and a carrier bag in the other. Dingbat the dog was sniffing around the carrier bag and thumping his tail on the ground.

"So, Twig," said Will, "are you ready to begin your training?"

"Well I've had some cheese," said Twig.

"I'll explain later," said Hooey as Will raised an eyebrow. "Tell him about the book, Will."

Will held up the book, which was called ***DON'T BE AFRAID, JUST FEEL THE FORCE***.

It was written by a woman called Frieda Frederickson and on the cover was a picture of a wall. In the middle of the wall was a hole shaped like a person, and a happy-looking woman was running away from it, leaving a trail of bricks in the road.

Will turned to one of the pages he had marked with a yellow sticker. "The question you should be asking yourself, Twig, is: **Are my actions moving me towards a more powerful place?**"

"Not really," said Twig, bending down to stroke Dingbat. "At the moment they're moving me towards Dingbat the dog."

"**To change your world**," Will went on, "**you must first deal with your fear. Say yes to life and become a woman of power and substance**."

Twig frowned.

"I'm not sure I want to do that," he said.

"Stay with it, Twig," said Hooey. "Frieda Frederickson says that **Winning is all in the mind**."

"Great," said Twig. "I'll just go home and think about it then."

"Wait," said Hooey, grabbing Dingbat by the collar and taking out a stopwatch.

"Why?" asked Twig.

"Because it's time to **face your fears**," said Will, taking a pack of streaky bacon from his bag. "**Your fears will make you stronger**."

"Page fifty-three?" said Hooey.

"Second paragraph," said Will.

"But I'm not scared of bacon," said Twig. "I quite like it actually."

Will cut holes in the bacon with some scissors, took a length of string from his pocket and threaded it through the middle. Then he walked over to Twig and tied it around his waist.

"OK," said Twig, "now you're just being weird."

"Stop worrying," said Hooey. "Frieda Frederickson says **Worry is the weight that won't let us win**. There's a whole chapter on it. With diagrams."

"OK, Twig, go and stand on the track," said Will.

Twig wandered over to the start of the track, where a wire fence marked the edge of the playing field. Beyond it was a steep hill with a river at the bottom. On hot summer days the fence was always lined with small children dreaming of swimming in the cool, clear water. They knew it wasn't allowed. But it didn't stop them standing there and dreaming about it.

"TWIG! Are you listening?"

"Sorry," said Twig. "I was thinking how nice it would be to go for a swim."

"Come on, Twig," said Will. "You have to *focus*."

"But everything's about food at the moment," said Twig. "First of all it was cheese. And now it's bacon. How's bacon going to help me win?"

"It's not about the bacon, Twig," said Will. "It's about the fear. Hooey?"

"Coming," said Hooey. He set his stopwatch to zero and stood behind Twig, still holding Dingbat by the collar. "OK," he said. "When I say 'GO!' you have to run as fast as you can towards the other end of the track. Got it?"

"Yeah, I've got it," said Twig. "But I still don't see what the bacon has to do with it."

"**Trust and you will triumph**," said Will.

"I don't remember that being in the book," said Hooey.

"I just made it up," said Will. He scratched his chin thoughtfully. "Maybe I should write my own stuff."

"Eighteen point two four seconds," said Hooey when Twig got back.

"Is that good?" asked Twig.

"Good, but not medal-winning," said Will. "As Frieda Frederickson says, **It's time to feel the fear.** Hooey, prepare to release the MAD DOG."

Twig looked at Dingbat, who was sitting on the grass, chewing his leg. "*Him?*"

"He might not look crazy now," said Hooey, "but you haven't seen him when someone nicks his breakfast."

Will nodded. **"Feel the fear**, Twig."

As Twig jogged half-heartedly up the track, Hooey let go of Dingbat's collar and he trotted beside Twig for a while before turning round and coming back again.

"Oh that's pathetic," said Will as Dingbat flopped down and went to sleep.

Hooey waited until Twig had sauntered to the end of the track and then clicked the stopwatch. "Twenty-two seconds."

Will shook his head. "You know what that means, don't you?"

"Plan B?"

"Exactly. How long have we got?"

Hooey looked at his watch. "About forty seconds."

"OK, stand on the starting line, Twig," said Will when Twig got back.

"Again? Why?"

"**TEN**," said Hooey, "**NINE** ..."

"Look, what's going on?"

"**EIGHT, SEVEN, SIX, FIVE** ..."

"Will? Hooey?"

"And ... here he is," said Hooey.

They all turned to see
a large, shaven-headed
man open the
gate and
walk into
the field.

He wore ripped
jeans and a tight
T-shirt and each
of his arms
was tattooed
with a fire-breathing dragon.
His biceps were the size of rugby balls
and they bulged with the effort of trying to
hold back the two huge, growling Alsatians
that were straining at the leash.

Twig turned white.

"Is that Basbo's *dad*?"

"Sure is," said Hooey. "He always brings his dogs down for a bit of exercise in the morning, doesn't he, Will?"

"Regular as clockwork," said Will. "But the funny thing is, he never feeds them until he gets them home again." He looked at Hooey and winked. "Reckon they must be feeling pretty hungry right now, don't you think, Hooey?"

"Reckon so," said Hooey. "Just imagine what they'd do for a BACON BUTTY."

"OH NO," said Twig, watching the dogs sniff the air as Basbo's dad bent down to unclip their leads. "Oh no, no, no…"

Hooey held up his stopwatch and patted Twig on the shoulder.

"All set then, Twig? After three…"

Twig turned to look at the dogs, who
had just worked out that the delicious
bacony smell was somehow connected
to his shorts.

The dogs snarled and bared their teeth.

Then they began to run.

"One," said Hooey, "two …"

Twig screamed and ran down the track
as if his pants were on fire.

"… THREE," said Hooey, squeezing the
button on his stopwatch.

The dogs raced after Twig, their ears flat
against their heads and their paws thumping
heavily on the dry track.

"I think this is the one," said Hooey as
they watched the top half of Twig's body
trying to keep up with his legs. "He really
seems to be making an effort this time."

Three-quarters of the way up the
track, one of the dogs launched itself at

Twig's backside. But with a surprising burst of speed Twig arched his back, put his hands on his bottom and pushed his bacony-bits out of harm's way. Hooey heard the dog's teeth snap at the empty air and then it tumbled off the track in a cloud of dust.

"ALL-RIGHT!"

cried Hooey, jumping up and down. "Go for it, Twiggy-boy!"

As the second dog snapped at his bottom, Twig seemed to step up a gear and took off like a rocket towards the end of the track. The dog, sensing its breakfast had laid down some kind of challenge, thrust its back legs as far between its front ones as it possibly could. It powered forwards and, even from where he was standing, Hooey could hear the **Grrrruuufff!** as it leapt into the air. Then, as Twig's trainers skidded across the finishing line, it bit him on the bottom, grabbed the bacon and tore a hole in the back of his shorts.

"TOUCHDOWN!" shouted
Hooey, pressing the button
on his stopwatch.

"YAAAARGH!"
shouted Twig,
sprinting back down
the track again.

"OI!" shouted Mr Basbo, shaking his fist.
"Stop picking on my frimpin' dogs,

y'little blimpers!

* * *

"Basbo's dad seemed a little upset,"
said Will as they stopped to catch their
breath on the seafront.

"Never mind him," said Twig. "What
about my shorts?"

Twig turned round to reveal a ragged hole
where the dog had ripped off the bacon.

Will looked more closely.

"Are you wearing your mum's
pants?" he asked.

"If you must know, someone got the presents mixed up at Christmas," said Twig. "But they're actually very comfy."

"Roomy too, by the look of it," said Hooey.

"I don't wish to discuss **my pants** thank you very much," said Twig. "I want to discuss the fact that you arranged for two massive Alsatians to bite me on the bum."

"Only one actually," said Hooey. "And on that subject, we have good news for you, don't we, Will?"

"Yes we do, Hooey."

Will opened his notebook. "Thanks to OPERATION MAD DOG, you ran the whole length of the track in fourteen point seven four seconds."

18.24
22.00
14.74

"Shweet," said Twig. "Can I go and change my shorts now?"

"Of course," said Hooey. "After all, you'll need to look good when you're a famous athlete."

Twig stopped and his eyes lit up. "D'you really think Samantha will like me if I win a gold medal?"

"Definitely," said Hooey. "Girls love
a winner, Twig.

WANGING THE WELLY

On the morning of Sports Day, everyone
in the class was very excited. Sarah-Jane
Silverton wore her gymnastics outfit complete
with leg warmers, Basbo wore a T-shirt with
NO TIME FOR LOSERS printed on it
and Samantha Curbitt wore a white polo shirt
with matching shorts and trainers.

"She looks like a Greek goddess," sighed
Twig. "A Greek goddess who shops in
Primark."

"Now then," said Miss Troutson, "I know you're all excited about Sports Day. But it's important we don't forget that this is all part of our topic. So who can tell me something about Ancient Greece. Sarah-Jane?"

"I found out that many Greek myths are about *love*, Miss Troutson."

"Yeuuch!" said Wayne. "Pass the bucket!"

"Be quiet, Wayne," said Miss Troutson as Twig looked longingly at Samantha.

"If you listen to Sarah-Jane, you might just learn something."

"Something about *luurve*," said Ashley Binkerton, fluttering his eyelashes and blowing kisses at Twig.

Twig waited until Miss Troutson wasn't looking, then pulled the rubber off the end of his pencil and threw it at Ashley. It hit the desk, bounced off his pencil case and got stuck up his left nostril.

"Hnff!" said Ashley in a surprised, rubber-up-the-nose kind of way.

Hnff, bnff!

"And you can be quiet as well, Ashley," said Miss Troutson. "Please, Sarah-Jane. Continue."

"Well, Orpheus was a wonderful musician who loved Eurydice, but after he married her she got bitten by a snake and died."

"**Mith Twout-thon, can I go and get a tith-yew?**" asked Ashley, holding his nose.

"Ignore him, Sarah-Jane," said Miss Troutson.

"Orpheus was so unhappy he went down to the underworld to beg Pluto to free her," Sarah-Jane continued. "Pluto said as long as he didn't look back, he could take her out. But he couldn't help himself and then some women called the Maenads came along and **RIPPED HIM APART.**"

"The Mynards?" said Dylan, looking up from his copy of *What Truck?* magazine.

"They live next door to my auntie." He turned to Martin Brimble and added, "Sounds like just the kind of thing they *would* do. Especially on a Friday night."

"I think we're getting off the subject here," said Miss Troutson. "But thank you, Sarah-Jane, that was most enlightening."

"Mith Twout-thon, pleath may I get a tith-yew?" said Ashley. "I think I've got a wubber thtuck up my noeth."

"Oh for goodness' sake, Ashley, yes, go on," said Miss Troutson irritably. "I've never known anyone make such a fuss."

"Hossitcomealong," said Basbo.

"I beg your pardon, Barry," said Miss Troutson. "Did you say something?"

Basbo chewed his lip and scratched his head.

"**Hossitcomealong**," he repeated. "Hossitcomealong annenna men all jumpout, annennay smashanfight, annennay chopperredsoff annat."

"*Ah yes*, the Trojan Horse," said Miss Troutson. "Well done, Barry."

"How did she get that from that?" asked Hooey.

"You get a feel for it after a while," said Twig. "It's a bit like learning French, but instead of a trip to Paris, you get a smack in the mouth."

"**Smiginnamoof!**" said Basbo, glaring across the classroom at Twig.

"See?" said Twig.

It's easy when you know how.

* * *

In the afternoon the teachers led their classes
out onto the field and made them sit by the
side of the running track. On the other side,
the parents camped out with their rugs and
picnic hampers. Some waved at their
children, some took photographs
and some lay snoring after a
particularly heavy lunch.

"Here you go, Twig,"
said Hooey, reaching
for his Tupperware box.
"Get some of this inside you."

He peeled back the lid and handed
Twig three lumps of feta cheese.

"I'm not hungry," said Twig.

"But look," said Hooey, "Samantha's
eating cheese."

He pointed at Samantha, who was
standing by the fence and picking
dainty crumbs of cheese from
a wheel of Camembert.

Twig held up his own
cheese, showed it to
Samantha and then
popped it in his mouth.

"We've got *so* much in
common," he said.

* * *

There were lots of other races before the
final gold medal events.

First the
children from
Reception
Class had to
get across

an obstacle course, crawling under nets
and running along the tops of benches.

The winner was a small
girl called Kayleigh
Hawkins who carried
on across the car park
until the deputy head
stopped her at the gate.

"I reckon she was off home to watch
In the Night Garden," said
Twig. "You never know
what those little scamps
will get up to next."

The next event was
the Egg and Spoon Race,
which was all going well
until Cyril Boothroyd
from Class Two turned
to wave at his mother and
tripped over his own legs. He was about
to pick his egg up when Olivia Basket from
Reception Class wandered onto the track
and bit the top off it.

"**HEY!**" cried Cyril. "Give me my egg back!"

There was a **crunching** sound and
Olivia smiled at him through a mouthful
of eggshell before setting off

up the track after the other
competitors.

Olivia's mother, Mrs Basket,
suddenly remembered that
she'd left Olivia's lunch box at
home on the kitchen table.

"DON'T PANIC, OLIVIA," she called, reaching into her picnic hamper, "Mummy's still got smoked salmon!"

As she ran up the track waving her Tupperware box, some of the other mums thought it was the start of the Mothers' Race and leapt up to join her, kicking off their shoes and scattering children in all directions.

"LADIES, PLEASE!" shouted the headteacher into the public address system.

RETURN TO YOUR PICNICS IMMEDIATELY!

Most of the mothers sauntered back to find their shoes, but Mrs Scott and Mrs Hamilton-Talbot were racing neck and neck and didn't stop until they hit the hedge by the temporary classrooms.

"What a barrow-load of jolly fun!" hooted Mrs Hamilton-Talbot as a dinner lady helped her out of the brambles. "Same again next year?"

* * *

After all the other classes had run their races, Mr Croft the headteacher handed the microphone to Miss Troutson.

"Hello, hello," she said. "Testing, testing, one, two, three..."

The microphone screeched a bit, then Mr Croft turned the volume down and mouthed "OK" to Miss Troutson in a supportive but *get-on-with-it* kind of way.

GOOD AFTERNOON, EVERYONE,

said Miss Troutson.

"Good afternoon, Miss Troutson," chorused the whole school, because that was what they were used to doing in assembly.

"Yeah, yeah, yah-dee-yah," said Miss Troutson. "Now I am pleased to announce that it is time for our special events to celebrate Class Four's topic on Ancient Greece. The winner of each event will be presented with a gold medal by Mr Papadopoulos, of ZORBA'S RESTAURANT, NUMBER TWELVE, THE HIGH STREET."

Mr Papadopoulos smiled and leaned in to the microphone. "Don't forget, ladies and gents, is two for one on a Thursday night." He cupped his hand to his ear and added, "My food is a-calling to you. It say: Come eat at Zorba's. Bring all of your friends!"

"Yes, thank you, Mr Papadopoulos," said Miss Troutson, snatching the microphone back. "Now the first event is Throwing the Javelin. At least, it was going to be the javelin, but for HEALTH AND SAFETY reasons the javelin has had to be replaced with a wellington boot."

"Wanging the Welly," said Twig. "Samantha should win this. She's been eating all that cheese."

First to go was Sarah-Jane Silverton. She picked up the welly, threw it about ten centimetres then dusted her hands together and sat down again.

"She's still sulking because Troutson wouldn't let her have an Olympic Dance-Off," explained Hooey.

Next up was Samantha. As she picked
up the welly and headed back towards the
fence, Twig put his hands to his cheeks.
"**OH NO**," he said. "She's going
the wrong way!"

"Relax," said Hooey.
"She's taking a run-up,
that's all."

Samantha thundered down the track so fast that for a moment everyone wondered if she'd got her events mixed up. But at the last minute she stopped and flung the welly so hard that it flew across the field and landed on the roof of Mrs Binkerton's Renault Espace.

"Samantha's *so* strong," said Twig.

Last to go was Wayne.

"I saw him eating **Cheesy Cheddars** earlier," said Twig. "Might just swing it for him."

Wayne picked up the welly and began spinning around, slowly at first, then faster and faster until the welly became nothing more than a blur. Just as it seemed he was about to drill himself into the ground, he let go and the welly sailed off in the direction of the school vegetable garden, where Mr Bilks was standing with another barrow-load of manure.

Whether it was chance or whether it was the faint whistling sound that made Mr Bilks turn around, no one could say. But at the exact moment that he did so, the wellington boot smacked him in the forehead and knocked him backwards into the wheelbarrow.

As the children cheered, Mr Croft the headteacher tried to point out that this was rather unkind. But the parents were so busy laughing that he couldn't make himself heard and he had to turn the microphone up to eight before everyone finally calmed down.

Next was Hooey's event, the **High Jump**. The bar was so high that Hooey could have walked underneath without bending his knees. He watched Marty Mills spring neatly over it and then turned to Twig. "This shouldn't take long," he said.

He waved to the crowd, took a run-up and jumped. As the bar clanged against his forehead he waved to the crowd again, smiled and walked back to his place.

"Nice work," said Will, who had been showing the teachers how to add up the scores more efficiently. "Very stylish."

"Thank you," said Hooey. "Now it's Twig's turn."

Twig walked over to the start of the hundred-metre race, where Miss Troutson was talking to the other runners.

"I'll say, 'On your marks, get set, go!'" she explained, grabbing Basbo by the back of the shorts as he started to run off down the track. "Now is everyone ready?"

Twig nodded.

Basbo chewed his knuckles.

Everyone crouched down, waiting for the signal.

"OK," said Miss Troutson.

GOING FOR GOLD

As soon as Miss Troutson shouted "GO" Twig leapt forward as if he'd been shot out of a cannon.

"You see?" said Will. "That's all you need to win: some cheese in your mouth, some advice from Frieda Frederickson and a packet of bacon on your bottom."

"Don't speak too soon," said Hooey. "Basbo's catching up with him."

It was true. Although Twig had made a fantastic start, Basbo was beginning to pull away from the others, closing the gap between them.

"Focus, Twig!" shouted Hooey. "Think Alsatians!"

Twig and Basbo were neck and neck now, ten metres from the line, when Hooey's words seemed to float into Twig's ears and set his trainers alight. With a kick of his heels he stepped up another gear and pulled away from Basbo once more.

"THAT'S IT!" cried Hooey enthusiastically as Twig approached the finish. "IMAGINE THE DOGS ARE COMING!"

Unfortunately for Twig, this was no longer something he had to imagine.

Just beyond the finishing line, Basbo's dad saw Twig running towards him. His two Alsatians, Bullet and Tyler, saw him too and it made them think about bacon. And bacon was something that Bullet and Tyler felt was very much missing from their lives.

"BULLET! TYLER! NO!" shouted Basbo's dad. But Bullet and Tyler were already pelting towards Twig, low, hungry growls coming from their throats.

Twig saw them and let out a small scream. Then he performed a rapid U-turn, which sent him straight through the middle of Miss Pinkerton-Potts's picnic.

"**HEY**!" shouted Miss Pinkerton-Potts, the School **HEALTH AND SAFETY** Governor. "You trod on my trifle!"

As the dogs snapped at his bottom, Twig increased his speed and looked up to see Samantha standing next to the wire fence, about to take a bite from her Camembert cheese.

Swerving slightly, Twig knocked the cheese from her hand, jumped the fence and then remembered too late that there was a very steep hill on the other side.

As his left foot
hit the top of the
hill, his right foot
decided it would
rather be up near his ear
and then, not wishing
to be left out, his face decided
to investigate a selection
of humps and bumps
on the ground.
As various parts of
his body set off in
different directions,
Twig found himself
bouncing at great
speed down the hill
towards the river.

Back on the school field, there was
a surge of excitement as everyone ran
to the fence for a better view.

"What about **HEALTH AND SAFETY**?" cried Miss Pinkerton-Potts.

"Never mind that!" cried Mr Papadopoulos as Samantha's Camembert bounced down the hill next to Twig. "What about **the cheese**?"

It was impossible for Twig to hear any of this, of course. Some said it was pure luck; others that it was the mark of a true champion. But whatever the reason, as he bounced off the riverbank, Twig twisted sideways, stretched out his hand and caught the Camembert neatly in midair. Then he hit the water with a loud **splash** and disappeared beneath the surface.

"Come on, little Twig-boy," whispered Mr Papadopoulos, clasping his hands to his chest. "Be a Cheesy Champion!"

The crowd held their breath.

Samantha stared at her empty lunch box.

Then Twig's arm appeared above the water holding the cheese aloft as if it was the sword of King Arthur, and Mr Papadopoulos cried:

HE HAVE IT! TWIG HAVE-A-THE CHEESE!

The crowd went wild, everyone cheering so loudly that Mr Bilks the caretaker quite forgot about being covered in manure and started clapping and cheering too.

In fact the only people who weren't cheering were Hooey, Will and Miss Pinkerton-Potts.

"He was so close," said Hooey as Twig clambered back up the hill, still holding the cheese. "Another few seconds and he'd have got that gold medal."

"Looks like he's going to get something from Miss Pinkerton-Potts instead," said Will.

Miss Pinkerton-Potts pushed her way through the crowd and pointed at Mr Croft, the headteacher.

THIS IS DISGRACEFUL!

she cried. "What about my trifle? And
what about **HEALTH AND SAFETY**?"
Immediately, the crowd fell silent.
Although Twig falling down the hill
had been exciting, a lady in a pink
dress shouting at the headteacher
was a rare treat not to be missed.

But before Mr Croft
could answer, Mr Papadopoulos
stepped forward and bowed politely.
"Is very bad what happen to your trifle,"
he said. "Is not good when food go in
world and have big accident. But maybe
I cheer you up. Maybe two-for-one
voucher for Zorba's bring happy smile
back to your face?"

"Well now…" said Miss Pinkerton-Potts.
"That is to say, I…"

"Please, no need for thank me," said Mr Papadopoulos, flashing a shiny-toothed smile at her. "Now as for the boy ..."

"*Uh-oh,*" whispered Hooey.

"... this boy," continued Mr Papadopoulos, turning to Twig and holding his arm up in the air, "... this boy, he a CHEESY-BIG HERO PERSON!"

The crowd gasped.

"*I am?*" said Twig, pulling bits of duckweed from his hair.

"Of *course* you are!" said Mr Papadopoulos, clasping him by the shoulders. "The world say it too dangerous. The world say it cannot be done. In fact" – and here Mr Papadopoulos's bottom lip quivered with emotion – "I tell people that maybe Cheesy Chase no more. But when you watch cheese roll, when you see cheese bounce, something inside you say, NO! Cheesy Chase LIVE FOR EVER! And you run and you jump and you follow cheesy-bounce all the way to victory!"

Mr Papadopoulos dabbed at his eyes with his handkerchief before composing himself and turning back to face the crowd.

"And this is why," he announced, reaching into his pocket, "I award gold medal for **Cheesy Chase Champion** to ... **TWIG-BOY!**"

"**HOORAY!**" shouted the crowd.

> **TWIG'S THE CHAMPION!**

shouted Samantha, leaning over and kissing Twig on the cheek. "The new **CHEESY CHAMPION OF SHRIMPTON-ON-SEA!**"

Twig blushed and smiled weakly.

Then he fainted.

* * *

"I think this gold-medal-winning is pretty easy really," said Twig as they came out of ZORBA'S with their free kebabs. "I might **go for gold** again next year."

"You can forget Sports Day," said Hooey. "We're entering you in the proper Olympics. With me and Will training you, that gold medal's as good as yours."

"Hooey's right," said Will. "But maybe you should take a break from training for a while, just to give your body a chance to recover."

"Suits me," said Twig.

As they turned the corner, Hooey said, "That's good advice, on the whole. But something tells me it's not going to happen."

"Why?" asked Twig. Then he gulped and turned pale.

"OK Will," said Hooey. "Have you got a plan?"

"As a matter of fact I do," said Will.

They watched as Basbo's dad's Alsatians, Bullet and Tyler, licked their lips and stared hungrily at the kebabs.

"First of all we're going to count to three. Then we're going to run faster than we've ever run in our lives."

"Sounds good to me," said Hooey. "ONE—"

"Actually that's probably enough," said Will.

139

As they sprinted
down the street, Hooey
threw his kebab over
his shoulder and,
although the dogs
stopped to eat it,
the three of them
kept on running,
faster and faster,
even when they had
left the dogs a long
way behind.

This was partly
because they were
worried the dogs
might start chasing
them again.

But mainly it
was because …

when he ran Twig made

little

squeaky

noises

at the back of his throat

and they were all laughing

much too hard

to stop.

STEVE VOAKE (also author of the Daisy Dawson series) was born in Midsomer Norton where he spent many years falling off walls, bikes and go-karts before he got older and realized he didn't bounce like he used to. When he was Headteacher of Kilmersdon School he tried to convince children that falling off walls, bikes and go-karts wasn't such a good idea, but no one really believed him. He now enjoys writing the Hooey Higgins stories and hasn't fallen off anything for over a week.

EMMA DODSON has always been inspired by silly stories and loves drawing scruffy little animals and children. She sometimes writes and illustrates her own silly stories – including *Badly Drawn Dog* and *Speckle the Spider*. As well as drawing and painting, Emma makes disgusting things for film and TV. If you've ever seen anyone on telly get a bucket of poo thrown on them or step in a pile of sick you can be fairly sure that she was responsible for making it. Emma also teaches Illustration at the University of Westminster where she gets to talk about more sensible things.